Ancient Greece
by
Adam Bushnell

Illustrated by Vince Reid

First Published
October 09 in Great Britain by

PUBLISHING

© **Adam Bushnell 2009**

A CIP record for this work is available from the British Library

ISBN-10: 1-905637-84-5
ISBN-13: 978-1-905637-84-3

Typeset by Educational Printing Services Limited

 Educational Printing Services Limited

E-mail: enquiries@eprint.co.uk   Website: www.eprint.co.uk

Contents

GOLDFINGER
(King Midas, Dionysius and Silenus)

King Midas loved gold. I don't mean he liked it an awful lot. I mean he *loved* gold.

He started every day counting his golden coins. Then he would polish his golden cups. Next he would walk through the palace looking at his paintings of golden sunsets on the wall. After that he would stroll through his garden admiring the golden flowers that grew there. Finally he would sit upon his golden throne for the rest of the day thinking about how he could get more gold.

* * *

One day there was a big fuss coming from the

corridor near to the throne room.

"I say!" shouted King Midas, "what's going on out there?!"

"Sorry, Your Majesty," answered one of the guards, "we were just bringing this old satyr to you."

The guards were holding the arms of a satyr called Silenus. Satyrs are strange creatures; they have the upper body of a human being but the legs and horns of a goat. The God of Nature, Pan, was a satyr and King Midas always had a soft spot for him as Pan brought gifts of golden wine whenever he visited King Midas.

"Why are you holding on to him like that?" asked the King.

"He was stealing flowers from your garden, Your Highness," replied the struggling guard.

"I'm sorry, Your Majesty," said Silenus, "I saw the beautiful gold shining on the flowers and just had to pick some to give to my dear little daughter."

"Ah, I see," smiled King Midas. "So you have a love for all things golden too, do you?"

"I love all things of beauty," answered the satyr.

"Let him go and leave us!" ordered King Midas.

The guards reluctantly let go and shuffled out of the door.

"And you have a daughter too, eh? I have a little girl of my own. It seems we have much in common my friend."

* * *

Silenus stayed at King Midas's palace for ten days and ten nights. The satyr and the King exchanged stories and songs. They ate and they drank. They had a grand old time.

Eventually Silenus said, "My friend King Midas, you have shown me great hospitality, and I will tell my master, the God Dionysius, the God of Wine. My master will be missing me so I must bid you farewell."

Silenus was true to his word and told Dionysius of King Midas's generosity. So Dionysius paid a visit to King Midas' palace. The God appeared in the throne room in a flash of golden light.

"King Midas," boomed Dionysius, **"you made my friend very welcome in your home. For that reason I will grant**

you one wish. What do you wish for?"

"Wow!" exclaimed King Midas. "A wish! Well, the thing that I love most in the world is gold. Hmm, yes, I've got it!

"I wish . . . that anything I touch . . . from now on . . . be turned into gold!"

"It is done."

Dionysius clapped his hands together and disappeared from the throne room in another flash of golden light.

King Midas looked at his hands. They didn't look any different. He stood and walked over to a table. There was a copper bowl with a bunch of grapes in it.

King Midas held out a shaky finger and pressed it gently against one of the red grapes.

FLASH!

It instantly turned to gold. Solid gold.

"Hoorah!!!" shrieked the King as he leapt up and down on the spot.

He then touched the copper plate.

FLASH!

It too turned to gold.

He held the whole bunch of grapes in his hand.

FLASH! FLASH! FLASH! FLASH! FLASH! FLASH! FLASH!

A whole bunch of solid gold grapes.

King Midas then ran all over the palace touching things as he went. He now had golden rugs, golden curtains, golden shoes, golden tables, golden chairs, even a golden bed. He rushed outside and turned the flowers into gold, the trees, the bushes, the grass. Everything gold.

King Midas sang and cheered and skipped into the palace. His daughter heard the commotion and ran up to her father.

"Daddy, what are you doing? You silly old king, give me a hug!"

She rushed towards King Midas, arms outstretched.

"NO!" he shouted.

But it was too late.

His daughter was turned to solid gold.

There, standing right in front of him was a golden statue of his daughter. With her arms still reaching out in front of her. Reaching for her father.

"NOOOOOOOOOOOOO!!!" wept King Midas. He sank to his knees and sobbed.

"Dionysius, hear me! Please hear me!" screamed the King. "Take the gift away! I don't want to see anything gold ever again!"

Dionysius appeared in a flash of golden light.

"Go to the river. Wash your hands. The gift will be gone."

Dionysius disappeared once more and King Midas rushed down to the riverbank and began to frantically wash his hands.

Once he had rubbed and scrubbed for what seemed like forever, the King stood and walked back towards the palace. He noticed that the trees were rustling in the wind. The flowers were nodding. The grass was swaying.

They were no longer gold.

King Midas sprinted into the palace where his daughter hugged him tightly.

"I shall throw a party to celebrate!" shouted King Midas, "Everyone is invited! Send word to everyone! The gods will all be invited; let Pan know, let Apollo know . . . but the guest of honour will be Dionysius!"

King Midas threw his party. But unfortunately he drank a bit too much of Dionysius's wine . . . and got into more trouble.

DONKEY'S EARS
(King Midas, Apollo and Pan)

In Greece, there lived a traveller. He went
from place to place seeing the sights and
meeting people. He would work when he had
to, but he preferred not to.

* * *

One day, he arrived at a town he had never
visited before. He spent the day walking the
streets until he arrived at the market place.
There, he saw the King of that town, King
Midas, riding past on a magnificent Arabian
horse. King Midas was dressed in expensive
robes and on top of his head he wore a
turban. Now, King Midas didn't wear the

turban for religious reasons. And it wasn't
a fashion accessory. So the traveller became
curious about the turban.

He went to a tavern, ordered a drink
and said to the barman, "Excuse me, but why
does your King wear that turban?"

"SSSHHHHH!!!!" screeched the
barman. "Don't mention the turban! King
Midas is very sensitive about it! He never
takes it off and if anyone questions him about
it . . . he chops their head off! Don't mention
the turban . . . *ever!*"

This made the traveller even more
curious and eventually he got a job in King
Midas's palace sweeping the floors.

* * *

One day, the traveller was sweeping a long
corridor when he heard strange singing
coming from along the way.
"DU-DU-DU-DOOO
DU-DU-DU-DOOO
DU-DU-DU-DOOBY-DOOBY-
DOOOOOOO!"
The traveller walked a little further,
stopped and listened.

"DU-DU-DU-DOOO
DU-DU-DU-DOOO
DU-DU-DU-DOOBY-DOOBY-
DOOOOOOO!"

The traveller realised that the singing
was coming from behind a closed door in
front of him.

He pressed his ear to the door and
listened again.

"DU-DU-DU-DOOO
DU-DU-DU-DOOO
DU-DU-DU-DOOBY-DOOBY-
DOOOOOOO!"

The traveller then peered through the
keyhole and saw that it was King Midas sat
in a bath and singing,

"DU-DU-DU-DOOO
DU-DU-DU-DOOO
DU-DU-DU-DOOBY-DOOBY-
DOOOOOOO!"

King Midas was shampooing his
hair as he sang and the traveller saw that
the King was not wearing his turban. The
traveller also saw *why* King Midas wore the
turban.

The King did not have a pair of ears
like you and I . . .

11

The King had *donkey's ears!*

"My goodness!" exclaimed the traveller to himself. "King Midas has got donkey's ears!"

He rushed out of the palace and into the tavern.

"Barman!" said the traveller. "Give me a drink quickly. I've had quite a shock! I know why your King wears that turban. You see King Midas . . ."

"SSSHHHHH!!!" screeched the barman. "Don't mention the turban! I've told you before! I don't want to know why he wears it! I want to keep my head on!"

"B – But I've got to tell someone!" moaned the traveller. He felt that this secret would burst out of him if he didn't tell someone.

"Well," said the barman, "why don't you go down to the riverbank, dig a hole and shout the secret into the hole? It'll make you feel better."

The traveller rushed to the riverbank and dug a hole with his hands like a dog. When it was about the size of a bucket, the traveller put his head inside the hole and shouted,

"KING MIDAS HAS GOT DONKEY'S EARS!!!"

The traveller felt good! It was such a relief to shout out the secret that he did it again,

"KING MIDAS HAS GOT DONKEY'S EARS!!!"

and again,

"KING MIDAS HAS GOT DONKEY'S EARS!!!"

and again,

"KING MIDAS HAS GOT DONKEY'S EARS!!!"

After he had shouted out the secret many times, the traveller went back to the palace to finish his work.

Eventually, the traveller decided to move on to another town to carry on exploring.

* * *

Many years passed. It was King Midas's sixtieth birthday coming up and he wanted to throw a party in his palace. Everyone in the town was to be invited.

King Midas sent for his musicians and

said, "Musicians, I want you to compose a piece of music about how wonderful I am. I want you to perform this at my birthday party."

"Of course Your Majesty," said the musicians, bowing low.

But as soon as the King had left them on their own, they looked at each other and said, "How are we going to do that?! The King is mean and nasty all of the time. He's always chopping off people's heads! How can we fill a whole song about how wonderful he is?!"

"I know!" said the flute player. "I'll perform a long flute solo in the middle of the song. That will take up some time!"

The musicians all agreed and began to compose the song immediately.

A few days passed and the day of the party had finally arrived. Everyone was gathered at the palace. The musicians began to get very nervous. No-one was more nervous than the flute player. He paced around the room and eventually put his flute down on the floor to get a drink from the buffet table.

When he walked back to the rest of the

musicians, he stepped onto his flute and with a CRACK the flute snapped in two.

"Oh no!" exclaimed the flute player. "Hang on, I might just have time to make a new one!" he added.

So the flute player ran down to the riverbank, took out his penknife, cut a reed that was growing there and carved a flute from the reed.

He then rushed back to the party but he had no time to test his flute as the musicians were about to perform their song.

King Midas sat on his throne and nodded to the musicians to begin.

"WACKA-WACKA-WACKA-WACKA-WACKA-WACKA-WOO!

King Midas is marvellous! King Midas is great! King Midas is brave!

WACKA-WACKA-WACKA-WACKA-WACKA-WACKA-WOO!

King Midas is fabulous! King Midas is good! King Midas is wise!

WACKA-WACKA-WACKA-WACKA-WACKA-WACKA-WOO!"

It was then time for the flute player to play his solo.

He brought the flute to his lips.

He blew into it . . . and out came,

"KING MIDAS HAS GOT DONKEY'S EARS!!!"

The flute player stopped, the musicians gaped, the crowd stared . . . King Midas glared and said, "What did you just say? Play it again!"

"WACKA-WACKA-WACKA-WACKA-WACKA-WACKA-WOO!

King Midas is marvellous! King Midas is great! King Midas is brave!

WACKA-WACKA-WACKA-WACKA-WACKA-WACKA-WOO!

King Midas is fabulous! King Midas is good! King Midas is wise!

WACKA-WACKA-WACKA-WACKA-WACKA-WACKA-WOO!"

The flute player then brought the flute to his lips, blew into it and out came,

"KING MIDAS HAS GOT DONKEY'S EARS!!!"

"Take that man away and chop off his head!" barked the King.

"W – W – What?!" stammered the flute player. "B – B – But it wasn't me, it was the flute!"

"Play my song again!" shouted King

Midas.

The flute was handed to the trombone player and the musicians started their song again,

"WACKA-WACKA-WACKA-WACKA-WACKA-WACKA-WOO!

King Midas is marvellous! King Midas is great! King Midas is brave!

WACKA-WACKA-WACKA-WACKA-WACKA-WACKA-WOO!

King Midas is fabulous! King Midas is good! King Midas is wise!

WACKA-WACKA-WACKA-WACKA-WACKA-WACKA-WOO!"

The trombone player brought the flute to his lips and out came,

"KING MIDAS HAS GOT DONKEY'S EARS!!!"

"Take that man away and chop off his head too!" barked the King.

The flute was handed to the guitarist . . . then the pianist . . . then the harpist . . . and even the man who played the triangle and each time was the same.

"Bring that flute to me!" ordered King Midas.

The flute was handed to the King, he

put it to his lips, blew into it and out came,

"KING MIDAS HAS GOT DONKEY'S EARS!!!"

The King leapt out of his throne and shouted,

"How is this possible?! I want everyone here questioned until I get answers!"

The King's guards questioned everyone at the party and eventually the barman was brought forward to King Midas.

The barman said, "Y – Your Majesty, I once met a traveller who said that he had discovered why you wore a turban. I told him not to tell anyone but rather he should dig a hole in the riverbank and shout the secret into it. That flute was made from a reed that must have grown at the riverbank and held the secret inside of it . . . until someone blew into it and repeated the secret for all to hear."

King Midas thought about this for a moment or two.

Then the barman said, "We all know your secret now Your Majesty. Can we look at your donkey's ears?"

King Midas nodded slowly. Then he began to unwrap the turban. The donkey's ears flapped out for all to see.

"Many years ago," began the King, "I agreed to judge whose music was the most beautiful; Pan the Nature God's music or Apollo the Sun God's music. I foolishly declared that Pan's pipes were sweeter sounding than Apollo's lyre. The Sun God told me that I was no better a judge than a donkey. He gave me these donkey's ears to prove it."

"I like them," said the barman, "I don't like my ears though. They're like saucers on my head. They're too big."

Suddenly someone at the back of the room shouted, "And I don't like my fingers; they look like spoons!"

Then someone else called out, "I don't like my nose . . . it's like a bird's beak!"

"And I've got a birthmark on my bum!"

King Midas soon realised that we all have things about ourselves that we don't like.

* * *

He stopped wearing the turban and let his donkey's ears flap out for all to see. He became a much nicer person and stopped chopping people's heads off.

21

In fact, donkey's ears became so fashionable in that town that they used to sell them on the market place for people to wear on their heads.

And everyone in the town lived happily ever after.

SPY KING
(King Sisyphus, Autolycus, Zeus, Aegina and Asopus)

King Sisyphus was a very clever man. He was so clever because he watched and he listened very carefully to everything anyone said. The King rarely spoke, but when he did, the words were carefully placed and always right.

King Sisyphus had great wisdom but he also had great wealth. His was the finest palace in Greece. He had fine vases, fine crowns, fine clothes and the finest herd of cattle anyone had ever seen.

These cows were beautiful animals; their horns were so polished they looked like they were made of silver, their hides were deep red in colour and the bells around their necks played the most beautiful music.

Near to King Sisyphus' palace lived Autolycus, the earthly son of the god Hermes. Autolycus had inherited his father's fast feet; he was the fastest runner on earth.

Autolycus would go for a morning jog around the palace each day. However, a morning jog for the son of Hermes meant fifty miles in less than ten minutes!

It was during these jogs that Autolycus decided to test King Sisyphus's powers of observation. Autolycus thought that he would use his speed and his strength to steal some of King Sisyphus's cows, disguise them and see if the King noticed.

Autolycus smiled. He turned his small garden into a pasture for the cows to graze in and prepared a huge bucket of white dye.

Then, late that night, Autolycus zoomed into King Sisyphus's palace ground, picked up a cow and zoomed back home.

Once there, Autolycus painted the cow white.

Then he stole another.

And another.

And another.

Until he had six of the King's cattle in his own back garden.

The next morning King Sisyphus was strolling through his grounds when the observant King realised that some of his cows were missing. He counted and asked his farmers where six of his cows could have gone. Of course, no-one knew the answer.

That night Autolycus stole another six cows in the same way.

And the next night.

And the night after that.

Everyone suspected Autolycus of stealing the King's cows but no-one could accuse the son of the God Hermes without any evidence. And no-one could gather any evidence as Autolycus was just too fast. Even with King Sisyphus's farmers on watch every night!

But the clever King had a plan. A plan to catch Autolycus red handed, or white handed at least, as he painted the King's cows!

The next morning, when six more cows had been stolen the night before, King Sisyphus knocked at Autolycus's door.

"You have *my* cattle in *your* garden," announced the King.

"I don't know what you mean," said Autolycus innocently.

The King and his guards marched right past Autolycus and into the back garden filled with white cows.

"My cows are white and yours are red," soothed Autolycus.

King Sisyphus said nothing but walked over to the nearest cow, lifted a hoof and revealed words written there:

"These cows belong to King Sisyphus."

Everyone gasped.

"But . . . But . . . But," stammered Autolycus.

King Sisyphus roared with laughter.

"Oh well done, Autolycus!" beamed King Sisyphus. "You almost had me there! I haven't had such fun in ages. Come back to my palace; we'll eat and drink and make merry!"

King Sisyphus and Autolycus went back to the palace for a feast that lasted for many days. The King and Autolycus became great friends and King Sisyphus's daughter fell in love with Autolycus as soon as she saw him.

They were married only a few days later and the feasting continued. (Years later they would have a son called Odysseus, who would become one of the greatest heroes that ever lived.)

Once the feasting was over, the King's daughter and Autolycus moved out of the palace and got a place of their own.

* * *

King Sisyphus became bored. He continued to watch and listen to everything anyone said. He began to make it his business to know everyone else's business. He hid behind large vases and listened to other people's private conversations. He skulked in shadows and behind curtains.

The once wise and clever King gradually became sneaky and devious.

One day, as the King was skulking through the streets outside of his palace trying to get

the latest gossip, he noticed the sea nymph
Aegina running from the beach into a cave
nearby.

King Sisyphus hid behind a rock and saw
Zeus, the King of the Gods, fly down from
his home, Mount Olympus, on a cloud. Zeus
looked this way and that way, and then
disappeared into the cave with Aegina.

King Sisyphus crept forward to listen and heard Zeus say,

"I love you Aegina with all my heart!"

"Blimey!" thought King Sisyphus. "The King of the Gods in love with a sea nymph! I'll bet her father won't be too happy about this!"

King Sisyphus chuckled to himself as he made his way home, happy with the gossip he had collected that day.

The next morning King Sisyphus had a visitor. Asopus, the River God, strode up to the King's throne looking angry.

"I know you see all things King Sisyphus," boomed Asopus. **"My daughter, Aegina, goes missing every day and won't tell me where she goes or who she goes with. Please, tell me if you know and I will reward your land with fresh flowing water to every home."**

King Sisyphus smiled. He loved knowing what others *wanted* to know and told Asopus everything.

Asopus was furious with his daughter for sneaking around with Zeus. The River God rushed down to the beach and saw Zeus flying back to Mount Olympus on his cloud. He also saw Aegina emerging from the cave.

When she saw her father, Aegina yelped and ran back to the sea. But Asopus hurled a magic spell at her and she instantly transformed into an island.

The island grew plants and flowers and eventually became one of the most beautiful places to visit of all the Greek islands, as it still is today.

Zeus, however, was furious. He had loved Aegina with all of his heart and now she was gone.

He sat on Mount Olympus burning with hatred for King Sisyphus, the Spy King that snitched.

And Zeus knew how to get his revenge, as you will find out in the next story . . .

CHEATING DEATH
(King Sisyphus, Hades and Hermes)

Zeus sat and brooded. Eventually he stood up and grinned.

The King of the Gods would have his revenge. He sent for his messenger, the God Hermes, and said,

"Go to Tartarus, the Underworld, and fetch me my brother."

Hermes leapt into the air, and thanks to his winged boots, he zoomed off as quick as lightning.

Zeus's brother, Hades, sat on his throne in the darkness of the Underworld. It was a gloomy place but Hades liked it that way. The sun gave him a headache and he liked to be on his own. The rest of the gods partied

and played on Mount Olympus but Hades just liked the company of the dead. They were much quieter, and fabulous listeners.

Hermes told Hades that Zeus wished to see him and the God of the Dead sighed.

"I'll get my sunglasses," he said wearily.

Hermes and Hades flew up to Mount Olympus, the light from the sun already bringing on one of Hades's migraines.

"Hades, my brother!" boomed Zeus, **"I want you to find King Sisyphus and drag him down to Tartarus. Throw him to your three headed dog, throw him into the River Styx, throw him wherever you like but make him *suffer*!"**

Hades nodded. He would have agreed to anything just to get out of that bright light; his head was pounding.

So Hades flew from Mount Olympus straight to King Sisyphus's palace.

King Sisyphus may have become a gossip and a spy but he wasn't stupid. He knew that Zeus would want revenge for what had happened to Aegina, so when Hades arrived in his throne room, the King wasn't the least bit surprised.

"Greetings Hades!" smiled King Sisyphus. "Welcome to my palace. Can I offer you food or drink?"

"**You know why I am here, King Sisyphus,**" Hades said gloomily while rubbing his forehead. "**Come on. You're coming with me.**"

But King Sisyphus pulled open the curtains to his throne room even wider, blinding the God of the Dead. Then the King pushed Hades onto the throne, took a long rope and tied the God to the throne.

Hades was powerless. Blinded by the sun, struck down by the worst headache of his eternal life!

King Sisyphus ran from his palace and hid in the cave that was once the secret hideout for Zeus and Aegina.

As night fell, Hades regained his strength. The God stood up, ropes falling at his feet and roared with anger.

He returned to the Underworld where Hermes was waiting for him.

"**Zeus wants to know what punishment you have set for King**

Sisyphus. Where is he? And where have you been?! I've been waiting here for ages!"

"I have the worst headache in the world. Sisyphus tricked me. Cheated *me*! He will have the worst punishment in the whole of Tartarus for that!" raged Hades, "I need to lie down. Bring him to me Hermes, while I decide the sneaky King's fate."

Hermes was glad to get out of the Underworld and flew to King Sisyphus's palace.

King Sisyphus had disguised himself as a beggar and set off along the streets near his palace. This didn't fool Hermes. The winged Messenger of the Gods grabbed King Sisyphus by the scruff of his neck and set off back to Tartarus.

But when they got there they had to cross the River Styx. The King had to pay the ferryman a golden coin for the journey, as that was the rule of the Underworld. King Sisyphus was dressed as a beggar, he had no money. The ferryman knew that this man was a king and refused to let him cross without money.

So Hermes sent King Sisyphus home.
The god had had enough of the gloomy
Underworld for one day, so he joined the
other gods for a party on Mount Olympus. At
this party Zeus fell in love once more with
someone else. This time the goddess Hera
was the object of his affections. So the King
of the Gods forgot all about Aegina *and* King
Sisyphus.

But Hades did not. He recovered his
strength and dragged King Sisyphus down to
Tartarus.

He showed the King a huge

underground mountain and pointed to a gigantic rock at the bottom.

"Push it to the top and I'll let you go."

King Sisyphus gulped.

He began to push the boulder with all his might.

He heaved. He pushed. He struggled for many days and many nights. Eventually the boulder was just about to reach the top when it rolled down to the bottom.

King Sisyphus had to start again.

But once he got the boulder to the top down it rolled.

Again.

And again.

And again.

And as far as I know the king is still pushing that boulder up the mountain even today.

THE WANNABE HERO
(Bellorophon, Pegasus, the Chimera and King Iobates)

While King Sisyphus was pushing the gigantic boulder, his grandson, Odysseus, had grown into a hero. Then he too had a son called Bellorophon.

Now, Bellorophon had a lot to live up to. His great grandfather, his grandfather and his father were famous for their heroic acts. Bellorophon knew that if he wanted to be a hero then he too would need to prove himself.

At that time King Iobates had a problem. A mixed up, mythical, monstrous problem. The Chimera!

The Chimera was a monster that had

the head of a lion, the tail of a snake, the body of a goat and could breathe fire like a dragon.

Many heroes had tried to defeat the Chimera but all had been burnt alive.

Bellorophon saw his chance; he strode into King Iobates's palace and spoke bravely, "I am here to kill the Chimera!"

"Ooooh!" squealed King Iobates, "You're so muscular! I'm sure that you're the man for the job! I'll tell you what; if you do defeat this monster then I'll give you a great big box of treasure AND I'll make sure that everyone hears what a handsome hero you are!"

Bellorophon thanked the King and strutted out of the palace feeling confident.

But Bellorophon was no fool; he knew that he needed help to kill the Chimera. So he went to see The Oracle, the wisest of all men in Greece. Bellorophon knocked at The Oracle's door.

The Oracle soon appeared smiling his toothless grin, "Hello Bellorophon me old mate, I haven't seen yer for ages, how yer doin'?"

"I need to know how to kill the Chimera!" boomed Bellorophon.

"Oh, no, no, no, no, no, no, no," The Oracle shook his head. "You don't want to do that. You see the Chimera has the head of a lion, so he can see in front of him. The tail of a snake so he can see behind him. The body of a goat, with a goat's head sticking out of his back, so he can see all around him, AND he can breathe fire like a dragon. The only way you would be able to even get close to that monster is if you could fly. Can you fly Bellorophon?"

"Erm, well, not really," answered Bellorophon.

"I'll tell you what," smiled The Oracle, "there's a winged horse called Pegasus that lands on top of that great big mountain over there every full moon. He goes there to drink from a crystal clear lake."

The Oracle then handed Bellorophon a golden saddle.

"If you manage to get this magic saddle on to Pegasus's back then he'll become like a pet."

Bellorophon thanked The Oracle and set off up the mountain.

Once there, he hid among the trees near the

lake and waited until night fell.

When the moon was full, Pegasus came flying through the night sky and landed for his drink.

Bellorophon crept up behind Pegasus with the golden saddle in his shaking hands.

Quick as a flash, the saddle was on Pegasus's back. Bellorophon took a step away as Pegasus turned to face him. Then Pegasus *bowed* to Bellorophon.

Bellorophon climbed onto Pegasus and they flew up into the air. The two spent the

rest of the night flying all over Greece.

In the morning, they flew to Bellorophon's house and collected five spears.
Then they took to the sky once more, searching for the Chimera. It didn't take them long to find the monster. It was burning down a farm nearby.

Pegasus swooped down from above and Bellorophon threw a spear at the Chimera. But, the goat's head looked up and saw them coming, so the Chimera turned its lion's head around, letting out a burst of flames. The spear exploded into splinters.

Pegasus circled around to the rear of the Chimera and Bellorophon threw three spears as quickly as he could. One after the other zoomed straight at the Chimera. But the snake's head saw them coming again, so the Chimera turned its lion's head around, letting out more flames. As the splinters of the three spears tumbled to the ground, Bellorophon knew that he needed another plan.

He pulled at Pegasus's reigns and they flew over and landed by a lead mine. Bellorophon jumped from the winged horse's back and ran inside the mine. He used his hands to dig into the earth and pulled out some of the squishy metal. He then pushed the lump of lead onto the end of his last spear and leapt back onto Pegasus's back.

The two zoomed through the air back to the Chimera. Bellorophon let the last spear fly and the Chimera let out a fiery blast. The spear exploded into splinters but the piece of

lead went straight into the Chimera's mouth, down its throat, into its belly and poisoned the monster.

With a thud the Chimera fell down . . . dead.

Bellorophon flew to King Iobates's palace and marched to the throne.

"Ooooh!" squealed King Iobates again. "You're back! I'm soooo proud of you, Bellorophon!"

The King kept his promise and rewarded Bellorophon with the box of treasure AND made it known to everyone in Greece that there was a new hero in town.

Bellorophon became so proud of his heroics that he decided that he was more like a god than just a hero. So he flew Pegasus up to the top of Mount Olympus. He then marched up to the throne of Zeus, King of the Gods, and stood heroically.

"My name is Bellorophon," he boomed, "and I am the greatest hero on Earth that has ever lived. You should make me a god!"

Zeus really didn't like being told what to do and liked Bellorophon even less, so the King of the Gods hurled a thunderbolt at the hero and Bellorophon blew up on the spot.

When Zeus saw Pegasus, the god liked the winged horse so much that he decided to keep him as a pet. This is where Pegasus still lives today, up in the clouds above our heads.

THE MAN-EATING MINOTAUR
(King Minos, Theseus, the Minotaur, Ariadne and King Aegeus)

King Minos had the most gruesome of pets. It was half man and half bull; it was the Minotaur!

The Minotaur didn't eat its five fruit and vegetables a day, it didn't even eat one a day, it only ever ate people.

King Minos had his greatest inventor, a man called Daedalus, design a maze that was built under the palace. This maze was an intricate labyrinth of tunnels that twisted and turned, this way and that. This was to be the Minotaur's home. It would live in the middle of the maze and King Minos would feed it with seven men and seven women every month.

The King and the Minotaur lived on an island called Crete, just off the coast of Greece. Each month the fourteen victims would be sent on a boat from Greece to the island and fed to the Minotaur.

Nobody in Greece dared to stand up to King Minos in case he waged war against them. The clever inventor, Daedalus, had made King Minos dreaded war machines that would crush an entire army. The people lived in fear of the terrible King.

In Greece, there lived another King; King Aegeus. He was as different to King Minos as could be. He was kind and generous, caring and fair.

King Aegeus had a son named Theseus. He was a brave and handsome lad . . . but not terribly clever.

One day Theseus went to see his father and said, "Dad, I don't think it's very fair that we have to send seven men and seven women to be fed to that dreadful Minotaur. King Minos must be stopped!

"I will be one of the seven men. I will travel to Crete on the boat, BUT I will take a sword with me ! I'll bet no-one has thought of doing that before!"

"Oh, my son!" beamed King Aegeus, "I'm so proud of you! Here, take this white flag. After you've killed the Minotaur, fly this flag from the top of your ship so that I will know that you have defeated the monster. Oh, my son!"

Theseus took his sword and the white flag and set sail to Crete with the other six men and seven women.

When they arrived at the island, King Minos's guards seized the sword from Theseus's hands and laughed, "Ha! Do you not think that people have brought swords with them before?! You big dafty. Now get into that maze!"

Theseus was thrown into the maze along with the others. It was dark. It was scary.

The other thirteen victims went off, one by one. Theseus could hear their screams in the darkness as each was devoured.

But then Theseus heard a different noise. He heard whispering.

"Theseus . . . Theseus . . . Theseus."

"Who's there?" called Theseus.

"It's me, Ariadne, I'm the King's daughter and I'm here to help," came the voice.

"Help me?!" asked a bewildered Theseus. "But you're the Princess of Crete! Why would you be helping me?"

"Well, it's my father, King Minos," replied Ariadne, "he's a big bully. I want you to kill that awful Minotaur. So I've brought you a sword . . . AND a ball of string!"

"Erm, thanks for the sword, but why would I want a ball of string?"

"Unwind the string as you walk the maze. I'll hold one end here at the entrance. Then after you have defeated the Minotaur you can follow the string to find your way back to me!"

"AAAAH!" smiled Theseus. "I like your thinking! But then what will you do? Your father will be furious when he finds out you've helped me."

"Yes, I know," said Ariadne coyly, "I thought that once you got back then perhaps we could run away together . . . and we could be married!"

Theseus thought, Well, she is a princess; she's bound to be beautiful!

"Yes, go on then!" he said.

So Theseus took the sword in one hand and unwound the string with the other as he explored the underground maze.

Eventually Theseus came to a room dimly lit by torches on the wall.

In the gloomy light he saw the Minotaur. It had the head of a bull and the very hairy body of a man.

The Minotaur snorted with rage, scratched the floor in front of it with a hoof, lowered its horns and charged.

Theseus wasn't too clever, but he was very fit. He rolled out of the way and the Minotaur snarled with fury. It snorted and charged. Theseus ducked and rolled. The Minotaur snorted and charged. Theseus ducked and rolled. Snorting, charging. Ducking, rolling.

Back and forth they went until at last the Minotaur was exhausted. Theseus then saw his chance and plunged the sword into the Minotaur's heart. The Minotaur collapsed dead on the floor.

Theseus then followed the string back to the entrance, grabbed Ariadne's hand and they were on board the ship in no time.

As they sailed across the sea, heading towards Greece, Theseus looked at his new bride to be. He noticed that she had one eye that looked at the other one. She had yellow teeth that stuck straight out. She had one long bushy eyebrow that grew in all directions. She had a full beard and a nose like a pink carrot.

Theseus thought, I'm not sure if I want to marry her now that I've seen her in the light of day.

"Erm, Ariadne," Theseus said slowly, "shall we stop off at that island over there and have a party to celebrate our wedding?"

"Oooh, go on then!" squealed Ariadne.

When they arrived at the island Theseus smiled and said, "Why don't you go that way and get the drinks. I'll go the other way and get the food. We can meet back here when we have everything for the party."

"Oooh, go on then!" squealed Ariadne.

As soon as she had gone Theseus sprinted to the boat and sailed off towards Greece. But he was in such a hurry that he forgot to fly the white flag that his father had given him.

King Aegeus stood on the beach waiting for his son to come home. When he saw Theseus's ship returning without the white flag flying he burst into tears fearing that his son had been eaten.

When Theseus's ship landed he saw his dad crying and said,

"What's the matter Dad? I've killed that terrible beast!"

When King Aegeus found out what Theseus had done to Ariadne he told his son he was grounded for a month.

Everyone else in Greece, celebrated the death of the Minotaur though, but fearfully waited to see what King Minos would do next . . .

THE ANGELS IN THE TOWER
(King Minos, Daedalus and Icarus)

"DEAD?!!!!" bellowed King Minos, "MY MINOTAUR IS DEAD?!!!"

The messenger had not wanted to deliver the news. King Minos was not the sort of king to deliver bad news to.

"And this is the work of that King Aegeus's son, is it?!" King Minos suddenly grinned. It was the sort of grin that a crocodile might make before it eats its prey.

"I know just what to do. Bring me Daedalus. He will invent something for me. Something truly terrible. Something that will show the Greeks that nobody stands up to me!"

When Daedalus learnt of the terrible

war machine he was to build he was
horrified. King Minos wanted a flying craft
that would drop fire onto villages, towns and
cities. Daedalus shuddered at the thought.
Thousands would die in excruciating pain.
How could someone think of creating such a
devastating thing?

Daedalus would not do it.

He had decided.

Enough was enough.

But how could anyone refuse King
Minos anything?

Daedalus began to pace the room.

He and his son Icarus had been
kidnapped over a year ago. They had been
happy working together in Daedalus's shop
selling his inventions until King Minos had
heard of these creations. The pair were
snatched in the night by King Minos's guards
and spirited away to the island of Crete.

They could come and go as they pleased
but were forbidden to leave the island. They
were prisoners.

Daedalus looked out from the window.
They lived in the tallest tower on the island.
It looked out over the tops of the gigantic
palace. It looked out over the sea. You could

even see the coastline of Greece on a clear day.

A pigeon landed on the window sill interrupting Daedalus's thoughts. It flew away immediately, leaving a single grey feather behind.

If only Daedalus and Icarus were free as birds to fly over the water and get back home.

Daedalus picked up the feather and turned it in his hands.

He smiled. He would make a flying invention after all. But it would not be the one that King Minos was expecting!

Icarus came home from fishing, holding his line looking glum. "Not a single bite today, Dad."

Daedalus looked up from his work. "Aha! That's perfect! Hand me your fishing line!"

Icarus looked at what was in his father's hands. It looked like a chariot had run over a very large seagull and there it sat; squashed and flat.

"What are you DOING?" asked Icarus.

"Making our escape!" beamed his father.

Daedalus held up his latest invention. It was a row of feathers held together with the wax from a candle.

"Erm, what's it meant to be?"

"Wings!"

"Wings?!" spluttered Icarus. "What for?"

"I want you to collect every feather you can find. Collect every piece of fishing line, twine, rope, string. Collect candles and beeswax. But do it all in secret! No-one must know!

"I'm making us a pair of wings each, Icarus! It's our only escape from this dreadful island and the dreaded King.

We don't have much time, two days at the most. Are you with me son?"

"Always," smiled Icarus.

In two days the wings were complete. King Minos trusted that Daedalus was busying himself making the flying craft that would spell revenge for the Greeks. His spies had told him that both Daedalus and Icarus had been collecting every feather on the island and the King was happy.

Daedalus used more melted wax to

attach the first pair of wings to Icarus's back. He then got his son to attach the other pair to his back too.

They looked at each other. The wings were folded flat against each other on their backs. Daedalus grinned.

"My greatest invention."

Icarus just smiled back, nervously.

"Now, we'll leap from the window. As soon as we do we must pull the two ropes at the bottom of the wings. That will stretch them out so they open fully. We'll catch the wind all the way to Greece.

"Health and safety first though! Don't pull the ropes again until we arrive at the mainland; if you do then the wings will fold and you'll fall. Don't fly too close to the sea; if the sea spray gets your wings wet then you won't be able to fly. Don't fly too high; if you get too close to the sun then the wax will melt and your wings will fall apart. Don't . . ."

But Icarus wasn't listening. He was looking out of the window, imagining taking that first step into nothing.

What if the wings didn't open? What if they came off his back? What if the guards shot them down with arrows? What if his father's invention just didn't work?

But that was silly. Daedalus's inventions always worked. Icarus trusted his father completely.

"You get all of that? Are you ready, son?"

Icarus smiled and said, "I'm ready, Dad."

Icarus stepped up to the window.

"You go first, son. If you have difficulty I'll be right next to you," said Daedalus.

Icarus closed his eyes, took a deep breath and stepped off the ledge. He opened his eyes and pulled the ropes.

The wings stretched open and Icarus soared into the sky.

"Wooooo-hoooooo!!!!" he screamed.

Daedalus followed and the pair glided past the palace and over the sea. He could just imagine the look on King Minos's face when he saw his prisoners escaping. Daedalus smiled.

Icarus was smiling too. It was the most amazing thing he had ever experienced. Flying. Really flying! Just like a bird! He tilted his shoulders and swooped this way and that way. He arched his back and soared higher into the sky. He pushed back his arms and flew faster.

"Remember what I said!" called Daedalus, "Don't . . ."

But Icarus wasn't listening again. He was zooming up into the sky doing loop the loops and laughing as he went.

He flew higher and higher until he felt the sweat dripping down his back. Icarus realised that he was very close to the sun and dipped his shoulders down to fly lower.

But it wasn't sweat that was dripping, it was wax.

The feathers began to float all around him in the air.

At first Icarus thought he was flying through a cloud but then he realised.

Suddenly the wings came apart like a feathery explosion and Icarus fell.

And fell.

And fell.

Daedalus watched as his son hit the water and he knew it was too late.

Icarus was dead.

Daedalus didn't make it to mainland Greece. He flew to the island of Sicily where he could live alone and mourn the death of his son. He didn't invent anything ever again.

But, when Daedalus died and arrived in the Underworld, the Kingdom of the Dead, he was reunited with his son and the two have been together ever since.

THE FIRE BREATHING BULL
(King Minos, King Eurystheus and Heracles)

"WHAAAAAAAAAATTTT???!!!" screamed King Minos, "MY INVENTOR HAS GONE??? FLOWN AWAY??? AAAARRRGGGHHHH!!! WHY IS THIS HAPPENING TO ME???!!!"

He charged around the palace smashing expensive vases and throwing plates at the servants' heads. After whacking a golden bowl over his chef, he began to feel better.

"Erm, Your Majesty," gulped the messenger, "I don't really know how to tell you this . . . but . . . erm . . ."

King Minos groaned and frowned. "*Just tell me,*" he hissed.

"Erm, well, there's a monster on the island. We don't know where he has come from. It's a gigantic bull. We've never seen anything like it."

"A bull?!" shouted the King. "You bother me with bulls?! Just kill the stupid animal and I'll eat it for my supper!"

"Erm, we've tried to kill it Your Highness. But it really is very, *very* big. Its horns are the size of columns, its legs are like tree trunks and . . . and . . . it can breathe fire. It's already burnt down half of the west wing of the palace and it's moving this way."

"That's it," sighed King Minos, "I'm going on holiday."

The King was packed and in his massive sailing boat in no time. He had decided to pay a visit to his good friend King Eurystheus on the mainland. They had met at an evil king party and been the best of pals ever since.

King Eurystheus and King Minos had so much in common. They both loved to beat their servants, feed people to monsters and bully those with weaker kingdoms than their own.

"Welcome my friend!" beamed King

Eurystheus when King Minos arrived. "You are very welcome AND you couldn't have come at a better time!"

"Oh, why's that then?" asked King Minos and the two kings smiled their crooked smiles.

"Come inside and I shall reveal all." They both gave sinister, evil laughs and stepped into the palace.

"The hero Heracles* is my cousin. He has been ordered to perform ten tasks for me by the goddess Hera. He upset her dreadfully but all the better for me. Bwa-ha-ha-ha! I'm having such fun choosing things for him to do. It's hilarious; I've had him wrestle with a lion, fight the nine headed hydra, capture a golden stag, ride a wild boar, clean out the stinkiest stables in the world and even do battle with bronze feathered eagles. It's been SUCH fun! Now my friend, you look like you need cheering up! Why don't *you* have a go? What would you have Heracles do?"

King Minos smiled his crocodile smile and said, "Well, I do have a little problem back on Crete. A giant, fire breathing bull is

*Heracles name was later changed to Hercules by the Romans.

rampaging around ruining my palace. Do you think your cousin could catch it for me?"

"Oh, of course. He won't mind a bit!" grinned King Eurystheus evilly.

"Oh, Heracles!!! . . . Ah, there you are my dear cousin. Would you be a treasure and go to Crete? There's a fire breathing bull there that I need you to capture. That OK with you?"

Heracles stood straight and said,

"Of course Your Majesty."

With that, the hero strode off to the harbour listening to evil laughs from the palace as he went. Heracles climbed into a little rowing boat and set off. The thing was, this hero had super strength. He was the earthly son of Zeus and possessed the strength of the gods. He climbed into a rowing boat and arrived on the island of Crete in less than three minutes!

Heracles saw smoke in the distance and ran towards it.

The fire breathing bull was wreaking havoc in the streets of the city of Cydonia. The city was scorched. Buildings burnt. Courtyards cooked. The people of Cydonia were rushing around this way and that way throwing buckets of water here and there. But it made no difference. Still the inferno raged.

King Minos's guards couldn't get near the bull; flames surrounded it, making it impossible to get close.

But Heracles knew what to do. He leapt into the air, over the flames and onto the bull's back. He then wrapped his arms around the bull's neck and began to choke him. The bull charged wildly, bucking up and down, up and down. But Heracles held fast. He gripped tighter and tighter, until eventually the bull collapsed to the floor and fell asleep.

Heracles rushed down to the harbour and took a huge anchor and chain from one of the ships there. He then wrapped the metal chain around the sleeping bull's neck so it was like a lead.

When the bull woke up, Heracles led it like a dog down to the harbour, put it on board one of King Minos's ships and sailed off back to mainland Greece.

Heracles led the bull into King Eurystheus's palace.

King Eurystheus and King Minos were

terrified when they saw the bull.

"Here you go cousin. One fire breathing bull caught, captured and delivered," smiled Heracles.

"AAAAARRRGGHHH!!!" screamed the kings.

"Take it away!" whimpered King Eurystheus, "Take it to the temple of Hera and give it to her as a gift!"

"Blimey," gasped King Minos, "I think I'm safer at home!"

So King Minos gave a shaky farewell to King Eurystheus and set off back to Crete.

When he got home he saw that not only his palace, but the whole of the island needed rebuilding.

"Why me?!" he moaned.

Also available from:

Invade and Settle, Raid and Meddle by Adam Bushnell
ISBN 978-1-905637-85-0

The Vikings and the Anglo Saxons; some of the meanest
and most menacing mad men that the world had ever
seen: they invaded, they settled, they raided and they
meddled . . . But what they did best was to tell stories.
Suitable for 9 – 12 year olds.

Snakes' Legs and Cows' Eggs by Adam Bushnell
ISBN 978-1-905637-21-8
Selected for the SLA Boys into Books (5-11) 2008 List.

Donkeys' Wings and Worms' Stings by Adam Bushnell
ISBN 978-1-905637-50-8

Fishes' Claws and Dinosaurs' Paws by Adam Bushnell
ISBN 978-1-905637-76-8

What happens when you sneeze with your eyes open? When
a woodcutter meets a dragon? When a giant wants a new
slave? Or when fire monsters try to keep the world feeling
icy?
The three books above include traditional tales and brand
new stories, each told with serious silliness. Each book
comprises of eight stories which bring together characters
from all over the world.
Suitable for 8 – 12 year olds.

Whispers in the Woods by Mark Bartholomew
ISBN 978-1-904904-61-8

Discovered lost in the woods and taken in by local
villagers, two mysterious green children find themselves
caught up in a quest to track down their missing father.
They encounter many strange and wonderful characters
but none are more terrifying than Silas of Wickham, the
witch finder who relentlessly pursues them to the sea.
Suitable for 9 year olds and above.

Chaos in the Cathedral by Mark Bartholomew
ISBN 978-1-904904-94-6

The quest of the green children continues as they search
the plague-ridden streets of Lincoln, looking for the one
man who can help them find Robin Hood who might be
their father. The children manage to escape the clutches
of the Master of the Lincoln Gilds and leave chaos in their
wake as they flee the quarantined cathedral before it's too
late! However, in Sherwood, one of them is captured . . .
Suitable for 9 year olds and above.

Swords in the Summer by Mark Bartholomew
ISBN 978-1-905637-31-7

Leaving Sherwood Forest and Robin Hood far behind them,
Fern, Hickory and Nathaniel ride west to the ancient
Celtic land of Cornwall. Here they must find the legendary
warrior known as the Green Knight, but Cornwall is in
the midst of war and the children soon find themselves
embroiled in a bitter struggle to defend the realm against
invasion . . .
Suitable for 9 year olds and above.

Beneath the Bomber's Moon by David Webb
ISBN 978-1-900818-33-9

It is October 1940 and the air raids have begun over
Thornley. Sparky and his best friend, John, like to spend
time with Sparky's uncle in the signal box at the train
station. One day they overhear the guards discussing the
two ammunition trains that have been hit, one in Coventry
and the other in Liverpool. The next one will soon be
passing through Thornley . . . will Thornley be a target?
Is information being passed to the Germans? If so, who is
doing it?
Suitable for 8 - 12 year olds.

Eye of the Storm by David Webb
ISBN 978-1-900818-56-8
Danny Sharpe didn't really want to go to the City Museum
in the first place. At the end of the afternoon, Mr Willis,
Danny's teacher, is desperate to get his class back to school
before a thunderstorm breaks out, but Danny has lost his
bag. When Danny wanders into the museum's Victorian
street, the storm breaks with full force, and Danny
embarks on the adventure of a lifetime . . .
Suitable for 8 - 12 year olds.

Bad Influence by Steven Lockyer
ISBN 978-1-904374-34-3
Polly Taylor is an intelligent, thoughtful 10-year-old, who
lives with her mum and moody older brother Chris. She
has an Uncle Jim, who asks her to look after a disk, and to
be careful . . . very careful. What he didn't tell her was that
it was dangerous and could change people's lives. Polly
being intrigued uses the disk and - oh dear, did she see
some changes!!!
Suitable for 9 - 13 year olds.

Watchers of the Sky by Stephanie Baudet
ISBN 978-1-904904-43-4

Since witnessing the plane crash in which Douglas Bader
lost his legs, Philip has admired the air ace as he copes
with such a disability. He himself suffers from dyslexia and
although no name has yet been given to it, he knows that
he is not as stupid as everyone thinks. Bader's true exploits
are relayed to Philip by his aircraft engineer father. Philip
prepares to leave school and hold down a part time job, as
well as coping with rationing, air raids and the discovery of
a German parachute . . .
Suitable for 9 -14 year olds

Moving On by Margaret Nash
ISBN 978-1-904904-42-7

Moving On is a story that begins in the late 1950s when
motorbikes and pop music were 'the thing'. The story is
loosely set in Liverpool amongst newly opened Wimpy
bars, Beatles' music, sky scraper buildings and the old pea-
souper fogs.
Suitable for 10 -14 year olds

Mrs Wrelton's Dinosaur by Ian MacDonald
ISBN 978-1-904374-48-0
Spike is a large, green, papier-mache dinosaur. He has
been in Mrs Wrelton's classroom for years and has always
answered the register! Until, that is, one day the class
have a clean up and Spike is seen in the rubbish skip. Sam,
Suhail and Amy set off on a dangerous adventure to save
Spike . . .
Suitable for 7 - 10 year olds.

Order online @ www.eprint.co.uk